THIS WALKER BOOK BELONGS TO:

_____

_____

_____

_____

For Melanie, Eva and Claudia

First published 1997 by Walker Books Ltd
87 Vauxhall Walk, London SE11 5HJ

This edition published 2002

2 4 6 8 10 9 7 5 3 1

© 1997 Clara Vulliamy

This book has been typeset in Century Old Style

Printed in Hong Kong

British Library Cataloguing in Publication Data:
a catalogue record for this book is
available from the British Library

ISBN 0-7445-8968-1

Two Friends

Clara Vulliamy

WALKER BOOKS

AND SUBSIDIARIES

LONDON · BOSTON · SYDNEY

Nida lived next door to Jake. There was a gap in the fence between their gardens,

just big enough for Nida to squeeze
through when she came to play.

"Let's go exploring at the end of your garden," said Nida. "It's a great big scary jungle down there! We can look for creepy-crawlies and put them in a jar. And maybe there's a tiger hiding in the bushes."

"We can make a tent and stay there for ever," said Jake, although he wasn't too sure he wanted to meet a tiger.

They packed Jake's rucksack with
all the things they would need.
They found a sheet to use as a tent,
and some blankets and cushions to
go inside it.

Nida fetched a fishing-net
from the toy box, in case
they needed to catch some
wild animals.

"I'll carry the fishing-net,"
said Jake.

"I had it first," said Nida.

Jake found the toy buggy for his
rabbit to ride in, and they set off for
the bottom of the garden.
Then Nida said, "It's Mouse's turn

to ride in the buggy. Give it to me."
She grabbed it and pulled.
"No, it's mine!" said Jake, hanging on.

The buggy toppled over ...

and so did Nida and Jake.

Jake ran off and hid in the bushes. He was cross and didn't want to share his things.

He watched Nida trying to make the
tent on her own.

Then he heard a rustling noise in the leaves.
It must be the tiger! Jake was very scared.
He ran to Nida as fast as he could.

"I can hear the tiger – it's there,
in the bushes!"
Nida was scared too.

As they stared at the place
where the noise was coming from,
out stepped Jake's old ginger cat.
He came lazily over and rubbed
against their legs, wanting to be stroked.

At last they managed to make their tent.

It was cosy and snug inside.

"I'm cooking sausages for our tea over the campfire," said Jake.

"And I'm keeping the wild animals away," said Nida. "This time we're looking out for CROCODILES!"

CLARA VULLIAMY studied Fine Art at The Ruskin, Oxford and the Royal Academy. Her illustrations have appeared in many leading publications, including the *Guardian*, for whose women's page she drew a year-long cartoon strip. Her illustrated children's books include *Ellen and Penguin and the New Baby*, *Danny's Duck* and *If I Were Bigger than Anyone*, which is a title in the Walker Maths Together series. The daughter of distinguished illustrator Shirley Hughes, Clara is married and lives in west London.

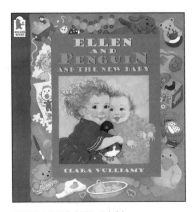

ISBN 0-7445-5252-4 (pb)

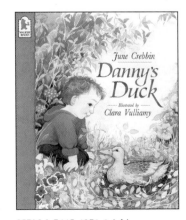

ISBN 0-7445-4371-1 (pb)